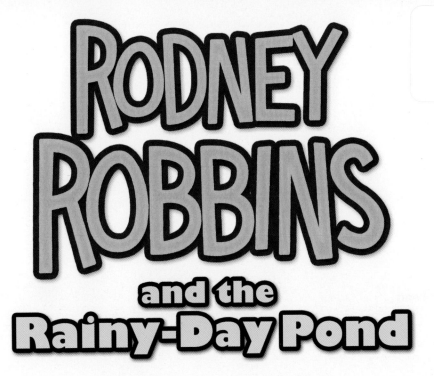

RODNEY ROBBINS
and the Rainy-Day Pond

Kim Stegall

Illustrated by
Bruce Day

journeyforth®

Greenville, South Carolina

Rodney Robbins and the Rainy-Day Pond

Written by Kim Stegall

Illustrated by Bruce Day

Design and page layout by Peter Crane

© 2010 by BJU Press

Greenville, SC 29614

JourneyForth Books is a division of BJU Press

ISBN 978-1-60682-058-2

15   14   13   12   11   10   9   8   7   6   5   4   3   2   1

In loving memory of
Grandpa Hamilton,
a reverent and gentle man
with a knack for problem solving
—KS

To my mom, Marian
—BD

Every time it rained, the street in front of Mr. Hamilton's tidy white house with the perfect picket fence became a pond. Not a puddle. Not a pool. A pond. Some folks called it a lake, but they were fond of exaggerating. And the pond was taking over the neighborhood.

One child lost a doll in the water; another lost a boomerang; and little Rodney Robbins, Mr. Hamilton's nearest neighbor, had nearly lost his brand-new Super-Duper Rocket Scooter with the optional flying-sparks feature.

The people on Colonial Avenue had tried for months to find someone to help solve the problem. Rodney's mother had called the City Works Department and the president of the home owner's association. Rodney had scootered to the mayor's office.

"I'd like to speak to Mayor Campbell, please. We have
a problem on Colonial Avenue. There's a hole . . . yes? Colonial. C-o-l-o-n-i-a-l.
Oh, yes, very patriotic . . . okay, I'll come back later."

One day after a big storm, Mr. Hamilton checked his cherry tree for damage. He was examining a broken branch when he noticed two red-sneakered feet protruding from a holly bush.

"Mr. Hamilton?" the voice belonging to the sneakers said.

"Ayuh," answered Mr. Hamilton, continuing to inspect his tree.

"I have another idea about the pond. A good one. I wanted to tell the mayor, but his secretary just asked me where my mother was." The body belonging to the voice appeared. "You wanna hear it?" asked Rodney.

"Ayuh," nodded Mr. Hamilton, cocking his head to one side.

And so it was that Mr. Hamilton, who had never protested much of anything, not even Mrs. Hamilton's tofu meatloaf, became convinced by little Rodney Robbins that something had to be done about the pond.

Minutes later Mr. Hamilton sent Rodney scootering home to ask his mother whether he and Mr. Hamilton could work on a special project. Soon the unlikely pair disappeared into Mr. Hamilton's cellar.

From all over the neighborhood, you could hear the *scritch-scratch*, *risp-rasp* of metal against wood followed by a *bang-bang-banging*. Paint smells wafted up the stairs and through the cellar door.

Mrs. Hamilton wiped her hands on her apron and called, "Mr. Hamilton! You and Rodney comin' up? Cookies almost done."

"Ayuh," Mr. Hamilton grunted as his head appeared in the doorway.

"We did it!" announced Rodney. The duo walked straight past Mrs. Hamilton's homemade wheat-germ-and-carob-chip cookies and out into the street. Mr. Hamilton was carrying a large wooden board with a stake nailed to it. His blue eyes were fixed, and his jaw was set.

Rodney carried a hammer in the back pocket of his blue jeans. And they both had fishing gaiters on.

When they reached the pond in the center of Colonial Avenue, the two paused ever so slightly before plunging into the water.

"Brrrr," said Rodney.

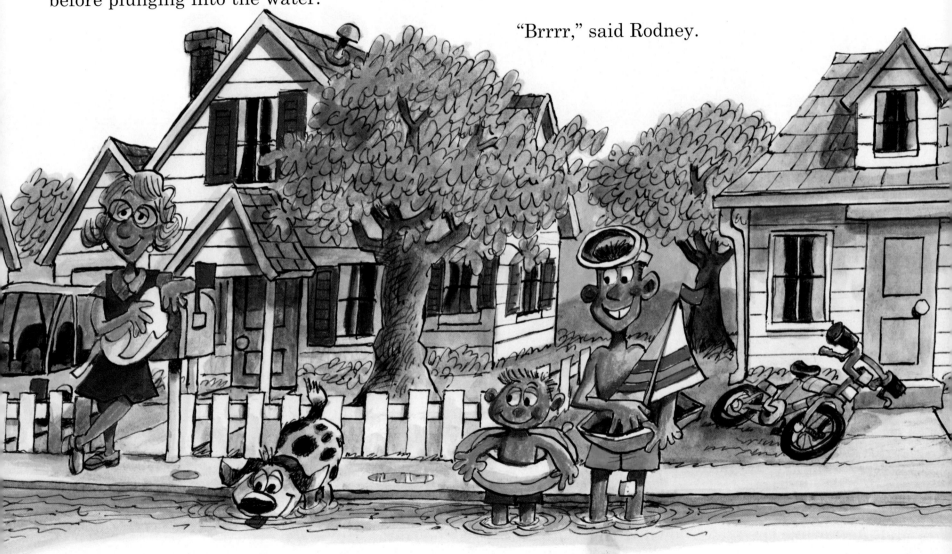

"Ayuh," said Mr. Hamilton. They walked until the water covered their boots, and then lapped at their shins.

Rodney handed the hammer to his partner. Mr. Hamilton held the hammer aloft and drove the stake down with as much force as he could. By now a crowd had gathered on the shores of Hamilton's Pond, as it had come to be called.

"What are they doing?" asked Miss Kelley.

"Rodney's up to something," said Mr. Jenkins.

"And Mr. Hamilton too," remarked Mrs. Elmore.

Mr. Hamilton finished pounding and went back to
inspecting his cherry tree. Rodney went back to scootering.

A roving reporter for the local paper was heading back to
his office from a fire across town. He took a back road from Elm Street to Oak Road
and found himself on Colonial Avenue just as Mr. Hamilton's sign was posted.

"Oh, boy," said the reporter, "a fresh local story is just what tomorrow's newspaper needs." He grabbed his camera from the back seat of his car and shot several photographs of Hamilton's Pond and the new sign sticking up from the center.

Next morning the neighborhood was buzzing with news. Everyone had seen the paper. You couldn't miss the story or the large picture of Hamilton's Pond and the sign that read: *No Swimming or Fishing Allowed.*

In the picture, cars were driving right over the yellow lines in the street to avoid the water, and bystanders were gawking at the strange sight of a fishing hole in the middle of a busy street. The reporter had even captured a boy falling off his bicycle while staring at the pond.

The following day word had spread to several neighboring communities. Folks from all over came to have a picture taken next to Hamilton's Pond. Some brought goggles or fishing gear to make the pictures seem more realistic. It had rained the night before, so the pond had risen even higher.

"What a great idea!" said a visitor from two towns away. "You could sell souvenir hats and key chains."

"Ayuh," observed Mr. Hamilton, who had ventured out to pull weeds.

"Or carrot juice," suggested Mrs. Hamilton, wiping her hands on her apron.

"Maybe," said Rodney.

On the morning of the third day, Mr. Hamilton was puttering in his petunias when
he heard a rustling in the holly and saw two red sneakers under the fence.

"Look, Mr. Hamilton," said Rodney Robbins pointing toward the center of Colonial Avenue.

Mr. Hamilton poked his head out from behind
a lilac bush to see three large pieces of equipment
descending on the pond. One looked as though it
would suck water; one had a load of fill dirt, and one
was preparing to lay asphalt.

A man wearing a yellow hard hat walked over to Mr. Hamilton's yard. "Sure sorry about all this commotion. We've been getting complaints for years about this mess, but no one seemed to pay much attention until this sign went up."

"Guess you'll be glad to see this crater filled in."

"Ayuh," agreed Mr. Hamilton.

"Whoopeeee!" hollered Rodney.

"You shoulda heard the Mayor this morning. He called our office himself and sent us out here right away. Said he didn't want to get one more email or visit about this *kerfuffle*, he called it."

The man in the hard hat went back to work, and Mr. Hamilton went back to his petunias.
Rodney remarked that the flowers looked especially nice this year against the Hamiltons' house.

"And thanks, Mr. Hamilton," said Rodney Robbins, "you're good at listening." And before Mr. Hamilton could say *Ayuh* . . .

Rodney pulled his Super-Duper Rocket Scooter with the optional flying-sparks feature out of the bushes and rode off toward the park.

Some time has passed now, and the new black asphalt has begun to fade to the steely gray of the street around it, but if you ever find yourself cutting through from Elm to Oak, you'll come to a large patch of pavement on Colonial Avenue that the whole neighborhood used to call "Hamilton's Pond." If you wave at Mr. Hamilton while he's out inspecting his cherry tree, you might just hear him call, "Ayuh," as you drive past. And don't be surprised if nearby you see a spray of sparks and a pair of red sneakers.